Arithmechicks
Take Away

Ann Marie Stephens

Illustrated by Jia Liu

ASTRA YOUNG READERS

AN IMPRINT OF ASTRA BOOKS FOR YOUNG READERS
New York

10 chicks in the coop.
Count their chatty beaks.
1-2-3-4-5-6-7-8-9-10.

They flap and play—
with their new friend Mouse—
far from their nighttime nests.
Then Mama squawks . . .

. . . "Time to hit the hay!"

No Way!

Chicks and Mouse huddle up.
Whisper, whisper, cheep, squeak.
These chicks are ready to subtract!
Take it away, Arithmechicks!

1 chick hightails it to hide from Mama.

10 chicks minus
1 chick equals . . .

9 chicks looking for cover.
Mouse hides too.

3 chicks hustle off.

9 chicks minus
3 chicks equals . . .

6 chicks fretting.

Mouse hides again.

4 chicks crawl down low.

6 chicks minus
4 chicks equals . . .

2 chicks panicking.

Find some place, quick!
You too, Mouse!

2 chicks split apart and climb up high.

2 chicks minus
2 chicks equals . . .

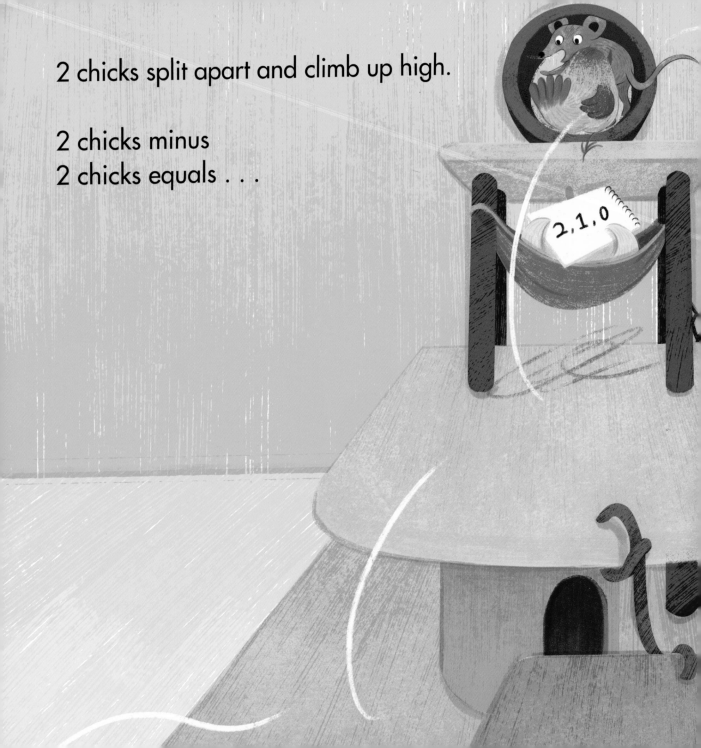

0 chicks left to disappear.

Shh! Don't make a sound, Mouse.

Mama squawks,
"Where have all my chickies gone?"
She doesn't see them.
She doesn't hear them.
Guess she'll have to find them.

Ready or not,
here comes Mama!

She spots a foot,

two tails,

and one giggly beak.

Then, with a little help . . .

. . . Mama tracks down Mouse
and the last 6 chicks.

She turns to lead the line to bed
when one chick shouts:
"Again! Again!"

2 chicks are first to vanish.

10 chicks minus
2 chicks equals . . .

8 chicks scrambling.

Mouse is on the move.

1 chick rolls away.

8 chicks minus
1 chick equals . . .

7 chicks flustered.

Mouse takes cover.

5 chicks tuck under.

7 chicks minus
5 chicks equals . . .

$7-5=2$

2 chicks choosing.
Hurry, Mouse, hurry!

1 chick barely squeezes in.

2 chicks minus
1 chick equals . . .

1 chick with no place to hide.

Ready or not,
here comes Mama!

1 lucky bird gets
a fluffy Mama hug.

9 other chicks want one too!
Feathers flap and feathers fly!

Feeling close and cozy
as their furry friend joins in.

All found and winding down,
with cuddles and bedtime books.

Stretching starts, yawns are next,
dreams are coming soon.

10 chicks in their nests.
Count their tired tails.
1-2-3-4-5-6-7-8-9-10.
And Mouse begins to snore.

The Arithmechicks love hiding around their coop because bedtime – chicks = later bedtime! There are many strategies for taking away numbers to get answers or differences. Here's how you can subtract too: Make groups of objects, such as blocks, twigs, or books. Then take away as many or as few as you want. Just like the chicks, you can write on a notepad or even use your finger to write in the air. Subtracting opportunities are all around you!

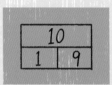

To **decompose** a number, or whole, means to break it into two parts. When one of the parts is subtracted from the whole, the one that remains is the difference or answer. This method is similar to a number bond.

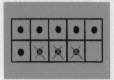

A **ten frame** is a visual tool containing ten squares. The dots represent the total number while the Xs represent the number that has been taken away. The remaining dots equal the difference or answer.

Fingers (or feathers) can be used to subtract numbers in an equation. Start with your hands showing the total number. Then fold down fingers as you are taking away the desired number. The fingers that remain are the difference or answer.

For my editor, Rebecca, who takes away my writing ~~misstaikes~~ mistakes —AMS

Thanks to my family for supporting me so that I can do what I love —JL

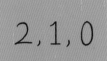

To **count back**, start with the largest number. Then continue to go lower by counting down as you take away the objects, pictures, or numbers.

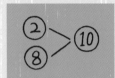

A **number bond** is a picture representation of a number and two parts that make up that number. It is a clear visual of the relationship between addition and subtraction. The large number is the "whole." The two smaller numbers are the "parts" of that whole. In subtraction, you take away one of the parts from the whole and the part that remains is the difference.

A **number line** is a line of numbers in sequential order. The first number in an equation is the starting point. The second number is taken away from the first by hopping spaces to the left, equaling the value of that number.

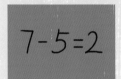

A subtraction **equation** is a number sentence that shows the difference between two numbers using a minus sign and an equal sign.

To **draw a picture** for subtraction, is to make an image to represent each number in the whole. Then cross off the desired amount to find the difference or answer.